A
B
C

| To_____ |
| From_____ |
| Date_____ |

D

E

Why Cody Can't Learn
By Mildred Joyce
©Copyright by Mildred Joyce, June 2007

ISBN: 0-9788985-1-6
978-0-9788985-1-9

A Better Be Write Publisher

For Information Contact:
A Better Be Write Publisher
PO Box 1577
Millville NJ 08332
856-825-6677
www.abetterbewrite.com

Book Cover and Illustrations by Jacqueline Kirk

Printed by Printing Systems

Printed in the United States of America

~Dedication~

This book is dedicated to my son Joshua, who is my inspiration. I also dedicate this book to my mother, Theresa; my father, Sam; and my sister, Betty.

I miss you all.

~Thank you~

Gratitude is expressed to all who gave freely of information, inspiration and encouragement.

Mildred

Why Cody Can't Learn

By Mildred Joyce
Illustrated by Jacqueline Kirk
A Better Be Write Publisher

Cody remembered the last time she was truly happy. She and her little brother were playing Cowboys and Indians. They were arguing about who shot who first.

Mother called, "Cody, come inside, it's time for you to learn your A, B, Cs and one, two, threes."

"All right!" said Cody, and she ran inside.

That was July 5, 1949.

Cody's mother tried to teach her the alphabet and how to count to one hundred before she entered the first grade. All her sisters and brothers had learned at that age.

Cody never learned all of them.
A, B, C, and one, two, three were as far as she ever got.

Her brothers and sisters said, "You're stupid. You can't even count to ten! When you try to do your A, B, Cs, all you say is A, B, C, A, B, C, A, B, C. You can't go any farther than A, B, C!" They all laughed, which wasn't very nice.

This was the first time Cody was teased. When Cody's mother tried to teach her, her brothers and sisters walked through the room. They always made fun of her as they went by.

Cody's mother ran them off at first saying, "Go away and leave us alone. Your teasing is not very nice when she is trying so hard to learn." But as time went by she said nothing to them anymore.

This did not bother Cody too much. *My mother can't teach me,* she thought. *When I enter school I will learn like my brothers and sisters. School is a special place where I will remember my A, B, Cs and 1, 2, 3s.*

On the first day of school the teacher, Mrs. Wiseman, said to each student, "Stand up and show me how much you know." When she got to Cody, she said, "Stand up, Cody. Show the class what they'll learn in the first grade."

Cody stood up and counted, "1, 2, 3 and A, B, C."

What else?" Cody did not answer her. Mrs. Wiseman said, "Why, Cody, all your brothers and sisters knew their alphabet and could count to a hundred when they entered school. Some of them could even read."

All this time I thought the teacher was going to teach me, Cody thought, crying inside.

Mrs. Wiseman tried to teach Cody. She did the same things over and over that Cody's mother had done.

Cody knew it was not going to work. She had thought the teacher would have another way of teaching her that would work.

Cody realized that school was no better than at home. She still couldn't learn anything. But now she had the whole class laughing and calling her names instead of just her sisters and brothers.

Only now if she didn't learn, she was spanked by her teacher!

Every morning the teacher said, "Get out the reader."
Cody's heart dropped to the floor. *Why does my day have to start with reading?* she asked herself.

Mrs. Wiseman said to the class, "Everyone, keep up. Each of you will read a paragraph. That includes you, too, Cody."

Cody knew that she was going to be spanked again in front of everyone.

Cody thought to herself, *How can I keep up? I don't know one word from another. I don't know how anyone can look at letters and know the words. And the teacher says* keep up. *I can't read this first grade book. I don't know the alphabet. I am so sick of this first grade reader. I just want to go home!*

When it was Cody's turn to read, Mrs. Wiseman had to tell her every word. Cody didn't know where she was on the page. She didn't say the words naturally. And to make matters worse, she stuttered now.

Mrs. Wiseman got out the speller. *Oh no, not the speller*, Cody thought. *Spelling is as bad as reading. I don't understand how anyone can remember the words and keep the letters in the right order. I **hate** spelling.*

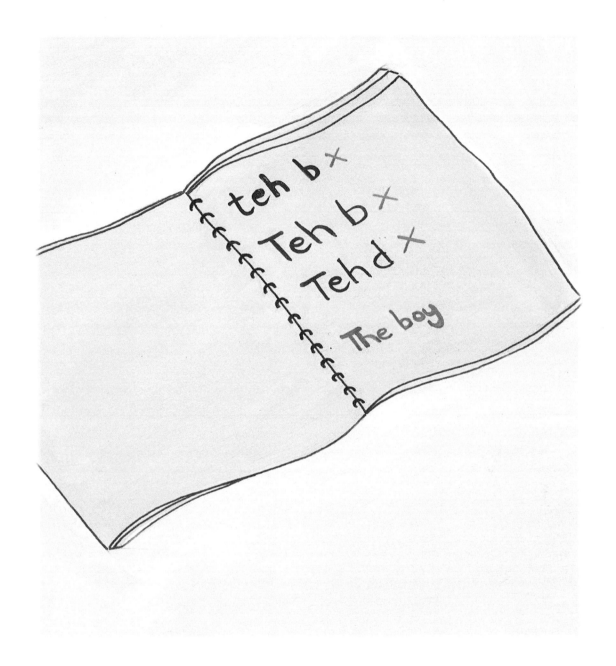

I'm trying to spell words that I can't read and I don't know the alphabet. I have trouble copying words off the blackboard. I get the letters all mixed up. How can I mess up just copying off the blackboard? She wondered, close to tears.

All this time Cody got spanked because she couldn't learn her alphabet, numbers, or how to read or spell. Mrs. Wiseman said, "You're not trying hard enough!"

Cody thought, *I don't dare say anything. Getting a smart mouth will make it worse. But I do not want to get hit again.* She began to cry.

Cody couldn't understand why after a year of school she had not learned anything. She could read some one and two letter words like "A", "I", "and", "or", "an", "the" and "to."

Cody had other problems, too: Sometimes when she talked about a boy, she would refer to him as "she" instead of "he." And sometimes when she talked about a girl, she would refer to her as "he" instead of "she."

She couldn't keep it straight. She knew the difference in her head, but she often said the wrong choice. Everyone looked at her funny and she learned to hate that look. She began to stay away from all the other children.

She didn't like to go places alone. She liked going places, just not alone because she got lost easily. "Let's stay together," she said to her one best friend, holding her hand.

Lunch was a good time for Cody. Getting there wasn't.

Mrs. Wiseman lined the class up by twos. She said to Cody, "I'll have to get someone to hold your hand."

Cody strayed out of line and off to one side embarrassed.

When Cody needed to go to the bathroom, she couldn't always remember the word, 'restroom.' She didn't want anyone to know she couldn't remember. She knew what it was but she just couldn't remember the right word. *Life is hard enough without everyone knowing I can't remember the names of things*, she thought to herself. She would just have to hold it and wait until the word came to her.

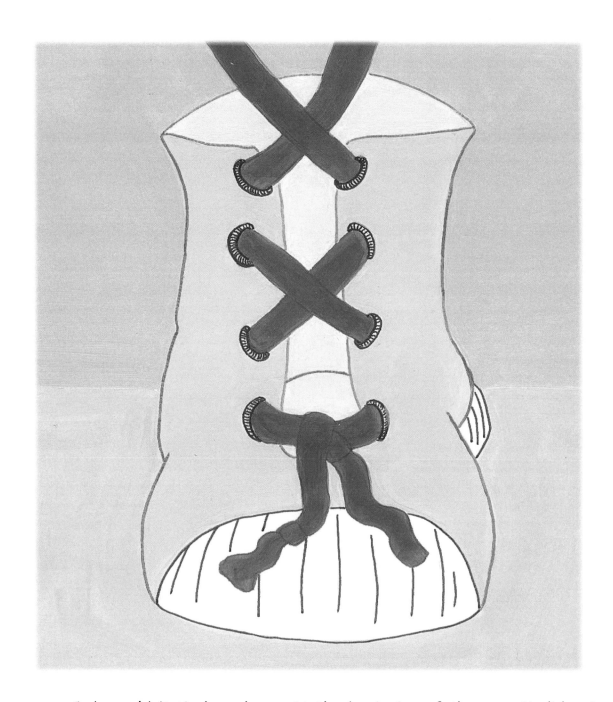

Cody couldn't tie her shoes. At the beginning of the year it did not matter because no one could tie their shoes. Now everyone knew how to do that except Cody. *I can't do anything right*, she thought.

Cody thought school was a special place where she would learn. She found out school was worse than trying to learn at home. There were more kids to pick on her. The days were very long. She was always spanked although she tried very hard. She hated school, hated her teacher, and hated all the kids except her best friend who did not tease her. She even felt bad that her friend was now also being teased for being Cody's friend.

The class received their report cards at the end of the year. Everyone was so excited. They had all passed.

Cody looked at the back of her report card. It didn't say the same thing as her classmates' report cards.

Cody asked Mrs. Wiseman, "What does my report card say?"

Mrs. Wiseman said, "Cody, you didn't pass. You will have to repeat the first grade."

Cody asked, with a tear in her eye, "You mean I have to do it all over again?" Mrs. Wiseman nodded her head yes.

Cody had looked forward to vacation and getting away from school. It wasn't that she really didn't like school. It was that school didn't like her. And she didn't want to be spanked anymore.

~Epilogue~

 This book was written to help individuals with dyslexia and others with learning disabilities to understand that they are not alone. Individuals with dyslexia--young and old--you are not mentally slow. You just have trouble learning things the way that others learn. Once you learn, you excel.

<u>Some Famous (and some about-to-be famous) Dyslexics</u>:

Albert Einstein, scientist; Leonardo Da Vinci, artist, architect, engineer and scientist; Thomas Edison, inventor; Augusta Rodin, sculptor; Woodrow Wilson, president; General George Patton, Commander U.S. Army; and Harvey Cushing, brain surgeon, writer.

Mildred Joyce, author of this and many other books.

Help Cody count: How many fishes' mouths do you see?

Can you name an object or two beginning with the first 20 letters of the alphabet? Help Cody find something beginning with "A" through "T."

Help Cody find the list of words by circling each one as you find it on the chart:

Clever	Ten	Garden	See	Seven
Yellow	Class	Crying	Done	Way
Help	Woe	Ear	One	Sad
First	Pen	Best	Two	Always
Grade	Test	File	Read	
Red	Toe	Cody	Nose	

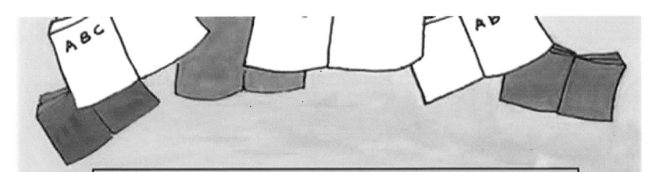

How much of the story do you remember?

1.   Who was Cody's teacher?

2.   What was Cody playing with her brother?

3.   Which word did she often forget at school?

4.   On which date was she truly happy?

5.   What is Cody's learning disability called?

Game 1
Answer: 13

Game 2

Apple	Ice	"Qq"
Book, Bottle	Juice, Jewelry	Rose
Cat	Knife, Kitten	Star fish
Dog	Lettuce, Leaf	Tail, Top hat, Tomato
Egg	Mushroom	
Fish, Fruit, Flower	Nest	
Grapes	Orange, Orange Juice	
Hat	Pencil	

Game 3

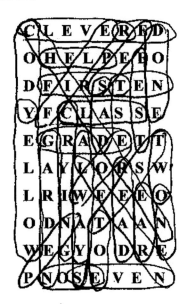

Game 4
1. Mrs. Wiseman
2. Cowboys and Indians
3. Restroom
4. July 5, 1949
5. Dyslexia